THE Night OF Las Posadas

Written and illustrated by

TOMIE DEPAOLA

PUFFIN BOOKS

For my New London friends, Fr. Dick Lower
and the parishioners of Our Lady of Fatima Church,
who were the first ones to hear this story;
for my Santa Fe friends, Alice Ann, Malcolm,
Christine, Davis, Susan, Jim, Ivan, and Allison;
for my L. A. friend, Roberto,
and most importantly, for my Mexican friend, Mario

Glossary

Farolitos • lanterns made of candles in paper bags

Luminarias • bonfires that light the way

Posada • inn

Santero maker • a wood carver who makes images of saints

Tía • aunt

Turistas • tourists

PUFFIN BOOKS
Published by the Penguin Group
Penguin Putnam Books for Young Readers,
345 Hudson Street, New York, New York 10014, U.S.A.
Penguin Books Ltd, 27 Wrights Lane, London W8 5TZ, England
Penguin Books Australia Ltd, Ringwood, Victoria, Australia
Penguin Books Canada Ltd, 10 Alcorn Avenue, Toronto, Ontario, Canada M4V 3B2
Penguin Books (N.Z.) Ltd, 182-190 Wairau Road, Auckland 10, New Zealand
Penguin Books Ltd, Registered Offices: Harmondsworth, Middlesex, England

First published in the United States of America by G. P. Putnam's Sons, a division of Penguin Putnam Books for Young Readers, 1999
Published by Puffin Books, a division of Penguin Putnam Books for Young Readers, 2001

20 19 18 17 16 15 14

THE LIBRARY OF CONGRESS HAS CATALOGED THE G. P. PUTNAM'S SONS EDITION AS FOLLOWS:
dePaola, Tomie. The night of Las Posadas / written and illustrated by Tomie dePaola. p. cm.
Summary: At the annual celebration of Las Posadas in old Santa Fe, the husband and wife slated to play Mary and Joseph are delayed by car trouble, but a mysterious couple appear who seem perfect for the part.
[1. Posadas (social custom)—Fiction. 2. Mary, Blessed Virgin, Saint—Fiction. 3. Joseph, Saint—Fiction. 4. Santa Fe (N.M.)—Fiction.] I. Title.
PZ7.D439Ni 1999 [E]—dc21 98-36405 CIP AC

This edition ISBN 978-0-698-11901-7

Printed in the United States of America

The artwork was done in acrylic on handmade watercolor paper.

INTRODUCTION

Las Posadas, an old Spanish custom which celebrates Mary and Joseph seeking shelter in Bethlehem on Christmas Eve, stems from the word *posada*, meaning "inn." It began in Spain and came to the New World, first to Mexico and then to the American Southwest.

In Santa Fe, New Mexico, where I have imagined my story, *luminarias* or *farolitos*, as they are called in New Mexico, line the edges of the Plaza in the historical district of the city. These candles placed in paper bags light the way for Mary and Joseph, the procession of candle bearers, and others singing traditional Spanish songs.

Along the way, the couple representing Mary and Joseph knock on doors, five in all. Each time a "devil" appears and tries to keep them out of the "inn." Everyone gathered in the Plaza boos the "devil," and the procession moves around the Plaza until they reach the Palace of Governors. There the gates are thrown open to a courtyard where everyone gathers and celebrates the coming of the baby Jesus.

—TdP

In a little village high in the mountains above Santa Fe, preparations for Las Posadas had been going on for weeks.

Sister Angie was so proud. Her niece, Lupe, and Lupe's new husband, Roberto, had been chosen to portray Maria and José—Mary and Joseph.

Sister Angie had been in charge of Las Posadas for years and years. It was she who trained the singers who followed Maria and José as they made their way around the Plaza in old Santa Fe and finally into the courtyard of the Palace of Governors, where an empty manger waited for the birth of the Holy Child.

"Now," Sister Angie said, speaking to the two men who would play the devils, "here's a picture of what your faces are going to look like." She wanted to make sure they knew how to paint their faces red with black eyebrows and beards, and that their red satin costumes were just right, especially the red capes and head caps with pointy red horns. The Devil would snarl and hiss as he tried to keep Maria and José from finding shelter. (The Plaza was so big that two devils were needed to rush from balcony to balcony without being seen by the crowd.)

Sister Angie always made the costumes for Maria and José herself. Blue and white for Maria, brown for José.

"Stand still," she told Roberto. "Lupe, I hope he isn't as fidgety at home."

"Oh, no, *Tía* Angie. He's just nervous about being José."

"Ah, well," Sister Angie said. "Let's just go to the church and look at Maria and José. They will give you inspiration, Roberto."

Miguel Ovideo, the *Santero* maker, had made a beautiful carving of Maria and José for the Golden Jubilee of Sister Angie the year before. Fifty years as a sister. Father Vasquez had put the carving in a place of honor in the church. As Christmas drew near, it was moved near the altar rail.

They stood looking up at Maria and José on their way to Bethlehem. "Just think of the carving and try to look like them," Sister Angie told them.

"I will," promised Roberto. "At least we don't have to worry about a burro."

Las Posadas didn't have a burro in the procession. Maria and José walked. The burro had only made problems, so they had stopped using one years ago.

Finally it was the night of Las Posadas. And Sister Angie came down with the flu.

"There is no way you can go tonight," the doctor told her. "Walking in all that cold weather—and they say that snow is coming. They will just have to get along without you this year." For the first time, Sister Angie would not be at Las Posadas.

"Don't worry, *Tía,*" Lupe told her. "We will make you proud this evening."

In the streets leading to the Plaza, men were busy putting the *farolitos* in place. They would be lit as soon as it got dark.

Wood for the bonfire was stacked in the courtyard just off the Plaza, ready to be set ablaze when Maria and José entered.

"Well," one of the men said, "it looks as if it will be a white Christmas. Snow is on the way." Even as he spoke, flakes drifted down. "But a little snow never stops Las Posadas."

Up in the village, the singers, the candlebearers—and the devils—piled into their cars. They wanted to get down the mountain before the snow, which was beginning to fall heavily. "Do you have the music?" "Where's my guitar?" "Wait, I forgot my gloves and earmuffs." "I'm so nervous." "It's a good thing you're not Maria. You'd faint." "Mi, mi, mi." "I hope my voice is loud enough. I've never sung the Devil before." It was the same every year.

Sister Angie looked out of her window. Yes, she wiped away a tear as she saw Roberto's old pickup pull up outside. Lupe and Roberto got out and rang the doorbell. They wanted Sister Angie to see them in their costumes.

"Ah, Maria and José. You look wonderful. If I had my way, I'd offer you shelter right here! Now, give me a kiss and be off."

Roberto and Lupe were the last to leave the village. Roberto's pickup had been acting up lately, and the deep snow didn't help. A sudden skid and the motor died. What to do?

"I'll walk ahead to see if I can get some help," Roberto told Lupe. "Wrap up and I'll be back before you know it."

Down in the town, everyone had gathered. The snow had tapered off and was falling gently. The *farolitos* were lit. The Plaza looked magical.

"Where are Lupe and Roberto?" Father Vasquez asked. "It's almost time to start."

The guitars were tuned, the horn player had warmed up, the singers were ready. Even the devils were ready. But no Roberto and Lupe. And everyone knows that you can't have Las Posadas without Maria and José.

Suddenly, down the street came a young couple. The man was leading a burro, carrying a young woman.

"We are friends of Sister Angie," the man said. "Roberto and Lupe are stuck in the snow on the mountain road, so we have come to take their place. We know what to do, and we thought our burro could be in the procession, too. My wife is going to have a baby and it would be better for her to ride."

"Let's go then," Father Vasquez said gratefully.

The candlebearers led the way, followed by Maria and José. The musicians followed and then came the singers. Out into the Plaza they went. Everyone knew their part, even the burro.

They stopped at the first door. "Oh, let the holy couple in—give them shelter—let Maria rest so that the Holy Child can be born," they sang.

José knocked with his staff. Maria looked down from the burro and smiled sweetly.

But the Devil appeared. "NO! NO! Don't let them in," he sang out. "Look at them—how poor, how wretched! They have no money." The crowd booed and shouted.

The procession moved on, knocking on one door after another. Sometimes the Devil popped out at them, and the crowd booed even louder. And sometimes they knocked, and no one answered.

It was one of the most beautiful Las Posadas ever held. Even the young woman playing Maria was about to be a mother just like the mother of the Holy Child. Perfect. They reached the gates to the courtyard. Once more they sang, asking to be let in.

This time no Devil. The gates opened wide.

The bonfire blazed, and everyone rushed in. A little pushing and shoving, but that was all right. Everyone wanted to be near the manger.

"Well, you certainly saved Las Posadas," Father Vasquez said, turning to thank the young couple who had taken Lupe and Roberto's place. But they were no where to be seen. Maybe they didn't know that they were to sit in the special place near the empty manger.

"Father Vasquez. We are so sorry to be late!" It was Lupe and Roberto, calling out as they rushed into the courtyard. "Did we ruin everything?"

"No, no," Father Vasquez said. "Sister Angie's friends were here. They led the procession, but now I can't find them. Go quickly and sit by the manger."

"What friends?" Lupe whispered to Roberto.

Sister Angie woke with a start. Las Posadas would be over. Everyone would be having their hot chocolate and cookies. The villagers would be back in an hour or two. I hope Lupe and Roberto did well, she thought.

Sister Angie was feeling so much better. She looked out of the window. The snow had almost stopped. Drifts covered the rooftops and the street below.

"I'll just go over to the church and light a candle," she said to herself. She bundled up and put the key to the church in her pocket.

Sister Angie crossed the street and stood in front of the church. Footprints in the snow on the steps led up to the door. She didn't think too much of it. Maybe some *turistas*—they came at all hours expecting the church to be open.

Inside, the church was dark except for the candle burning in front of the Blessed Sacrament. "I'll light a candle in front of the carving," she said. She took an unlit candle and struck a match. The candle flared up and settled into a steady glow.

Sister Angie knelt down and placed her candle in front of the carving. “Oh, Maria. Oh, José,” she prayed, eyes closed, “my heart will always be open to you so that the Holy Child will have a place to be born.”

Sister Angie opened her eyes. There, in front of her, she saw wet footprints leading to the carving. She looked up.

The cloaks of Maria and José were covered in fresh snow.

A Note From The Author

In Spain, as in Mexico, Las Posadas is celebrated for nine days. Families walk in procession, knocking on doors, but only on Christmas Eve does a door open, everyone enters and has hot chocolate and cookies to commemorate the expected birth of the Holy Child.

In San Antonio, Texas, a procession of boats, with the couple representing Mary and Joseph sitting in the first boat followed by boats filled with people singing, winds down the river that runs through the center of the city.

In Santa Fe, the procession is usually made up of people from Santa Cruz, a small village north of the city. It is a great honor to be chosen to play Mary and Joseph.

When they knock on the doors, a song is sung each time asking for Mary and Joseph to be let in. But the "devil" appears with an answering song to keep them out. It is very dramatic and even amusing as the crowds of people filling the square boo and hiss at the "devil."

Finally, when everyone has gathered in the courtyard, as in Spain and Mexico, hot chocolate and cookies are served.